The choices we make, the actions we take, the moments—both big and small—shape us into

FORCES OF DESTINY.

TALES OF HOPE & COURAGE

Why hello there, young one.

OF COURSE, WHEN YOU HAVE LIVED AS LONG AS
I HAVE, EVERYONE SEEMS VERY YOUNG.

I do not know how you have found my journal, but I'm glad that you did. **YOU DON'T GET TO BE OVER 1,000 YEARS OLD WITHOUT SEEING SOME AMAZING THINGS.** And sharing those experiences with others, well, it's a little like getting to relive them all over again for the first time. Have you ever seen the **FORBIDDEN GARDENS OF NUSWATTA?** Or perhaps heard the beautiful music of the **CATHEDRAL OF WINDS?**

NO?

Well, don't worry. You still have time. As you travel through this beautiful galaxy, you will see many wondrous things and meet many astonishing people. And when you do, take a moment to write it all down. As life happens around you, it can feel random or even cruel. But if you reflect, you will begin to see the shape of your own story. You will see how **THE FORCE** has helped shape the person you have become.

You do not believe me? You think your life too small to be shaped by the Force?

CHILD, NO MATTER WHERE WE COME FROM OR HOW HUMBLE OUR STORIES MAY SEEM, EACH ONE OF US CAN BE A FORCE OF DESTINY.

I'll prove it to you. Let me share with you the stories of six heroes. In their lives, each of these heroes would change the galaxy. But those are not the stories I am going to tell you. No, I will tell you of the times when they faced more ordinary challenges, yet they rose to each occasion with extraordinary talent, proving that they were **WORTHY AND DESTINED FOR GREATNESS**....

Let me start
with the story of

PRINCESS LEIA ORGANA.

You may know that she
was not born a princess,
but was the daughter of
a brilliant senator and
a POWERFUL Jedi.
Although her birth parents' story
ended in sadness, she was adopted by a
kind and loving couple:

QUEEN BREHA AND VICEROY BAIL OF ALDERAAN.

As Leia grew up, it was clear that she was a **NATURAL LEADER.**

Her parents knew this ability would serve her well when she took the throne one day, but they feared her abilities would be tested far sooner than her coronation. The forces of the evil **GALACTIC EMPIRE** were growing stronger. If no one stood against them and their quest for power, the entire galaxy would soon be under their control.

AREN'T THEY A **LOVELY** FAMILY?

And so, when Leia was just sixteen years old, she became the **YOUNGEST LEADER** ever chosen for the Galactic Senate. She fought the Empire by speaking out against their terrible deeds. When her words were ignored, she began leading missions to bring food and supplies to those hurt by the Empire. And when even that was no longer enough, she joined the

REBEL ALLIANCE.

In the Rebellion, Leia's gift for strategy helped them win many victories against the Empire. She even helped deliver the secret plans for the Death Star into the hands of the Rebellion with R2-D2's help. With those plans, rebel pilots were able to **ATTACK AND DESTROY** the Empire's deadly battle station. But for every victory the Rebellion won, **THE EMPIRE FOUGHT BACK EVEN HARDER.**

THOSE WHO WISH TO HURT OTHERS OFTEN HIDE BEHIND POWERFUL WEAPONS.

If you are something very small fighting against something very big, finding a good place to hide is important.

AS LONG AS THE EMPIRE DIDN'T KNOW WHERE TO FIND THEM, THE REBELLION WOULD BE SAFE.

But building a secret base can be hard work, especially if that base is on a cold, snowy planet on the Outer Rim. But it was Hoth's constant blizzards and distant location that made it a perfect base for the Rebellion. Think back to a time when you were very cold. . . . Perhaps you forgot your coat on a chilly day? Or perhaps you had just drunk an icy glass of bantha milk? Well, Hoth was **SO COLD** that even your thoughts might start to shiver!

(I WOULD HAVE RECOMMENDED **PLENTY** OF BLANKETS AND HOT CHOCOLATE.)

To keep everyone from turning into rebel-shaped icicles, Leia and the Rebellion leaders decided to build their base deep underground.

Digging out the snowy tunnels was hard work, but Leia's team had made quick progress. Now they were ready to finish off the last of the storage chambers and stock them with supplies.

Waiting on delivery in the next supply shipment:
- Bacta patches
- Field rations
- Nerf-wool blankets
- Instant caf
- Astromech power cells
(for R2!)

Leia's friend Chewbacca had volunteered to help dig out one of the last tunnels. With his strong arms, that dear Wookiee would be able to clear a path within hours. While Chewbacca worked, Leia saw to it that supplies were delivered in **PERFECT CONDITION.**

Then, she met with General Rieekan, the leader of the base, to talk through a few last-minute changes to their defense strategy. There was always a chance the Empire could attack at any moment.

Together, Leia and General Rieekan walked to the command center, speaking in hushed voices about their plans.

Their tense whispers were interrupted by a shout as they walked through the hangar bay. It was Leia's friend Luke Skywalker. And he had a **TROUBLING QUESTION.**

"Have you seen Chewie?" he asked the princess.

Chewbacca had offered to help Luke repair his snowspeeder once he was done with his work digging, but the faithful Wookiee was **OVER TWO HOURS LATE.**

Now, let me tell you:

CHEWBACCA IS NEVER LATE.

He could be caught in the middle of an ion storm on the far side of Wild Space, and he'd still be sure to deliver your shipment of blumfruit juice right on schedule.

(SOME OF MY CUSTOMERS ARE VERY SERIOUS ABOUT THEIR BLUMFRUIT JUICE.)

EXTENDABLE AUXILIARY VISUAL IMAGING SYSTEM

SCANNING ARRAY

LOCOMOTION POWER CELLS

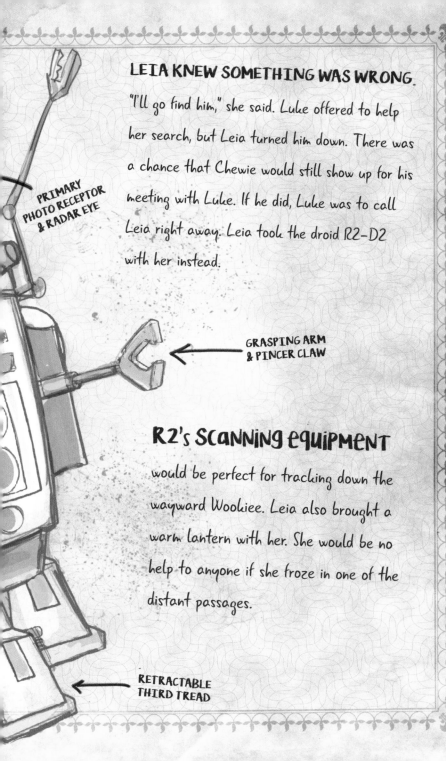

LEIA KNEW SOMETHING WAS WRONG.

"I'll go find him," she said. Luke offered to help her search, but Leia turned him down. There was a chance that Chewie would still show up for his meeting with Luke. If he did, Luke was to call Leia right away. Leia took the droid R2-D2 with her instead.

PRIMARY
PHOTO RECEPTOR
& RADAR EYE

GRASPING ARM
& PINCER CLAW

R2's SCANNING EQUIPMENT

would be perfect for tracking down the wayward Wookiee. Leia also brought a warm lantern with her. She would be no help to anyone if she froze in one of the distant passages.

RETRACTABLE
THIRD TREAD

With each turn, the passage grew dimmer and dimmer as
Leia and R2 got farther and farther away from the hangar.
At one junction, the endless white walls were interrupted
by a metal door frame, fallen on its side.

Nearby was a case of tools that looked like they had been left in a hurry. Leia was starting to get worried. **"CHEWIE!"** she called out. But her voice, muffled by the thick walls of snow surrounding her, didn't travel far. She walked quickly down another branching hallway.

"CHEWIE!"
she shouted again.
"PLEASE BE ALL RIGHT,"
she added to herself.

Leia turned to R2 to check his scanner, when she heard a faint roar to her left. That certainly sounded like Chewbacca! But what was keeping him from her? Had there been a cave in? **OR WAS CHEWIE HURT?**

Leia and R2 headed toward Chewbacca's fading howl. As she turned a corner, Leia was relieved to see the towering shape of her Wookiee friend.

He was crouching next to a big pile of snow, but as far as Leia could tell he was unharmed.

AND A GOOD THING, TOO!

I would have a few strong words for anyone who dared hurt Chewbacca!

HE WAS ALWAYS A FRIEND TO ME, TOO.

When Chewbacca saw Leia, he shook his head and gestured toward the snow mound. It was then that Leia realized that the snow was . . . breathing? Suddenly, Leia understood what was happening.

THE SNOW PILE WAS IN FACT A **WAMPA**—ONE OF THE FEARSOME BEASTS THAT LIVE ON HOTH.

LUKE SKYWALKER

INCOMING TRANSMISSION:

C-3PO

Your Royal Highness,

I regret to inform you that my repeated requests for additional heat lanterns in the command center have been ignored. Due to the long hours I must spend in the frightfully chilly room attending your majesty, my complex circuitry simply cannot withstand the continued chill. In addition to this request, I've included some brief thoughts here about how other systems on Echo Base could be improved. . . .

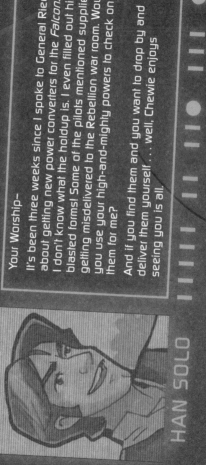

HAN SOLO

Your Worship—

It's been three weeks since I spoke to General Rieekan about getting new power converters for the *Falcon*. I don't know what the holdup is. I even filled out his blasted forms! Some of the pilots mentioned supplies getting misdelivered to the Rebellion war room. Would you use your high-and-mighty powers to check on them for me?

And if you find them and you want to drop by and deliver them yourself . . . well, Chewie enjoys seeing you is all.

Dear Leia,

I've attached the drill reports you requested on all of our pilots. Rogue Group is getting better every day. I think with a bit more practice, we could even shave a few more seconds off of our launch times. We can go over the full report at our next strategy meeting

Leia looked around the cavern and immediately came up with a plan. As long as the wampa stayed asleep, **THEY WERE SAFE**. She motioned to Chewie, encouraging him to slide silently across the icy floor, away from the beast. But before the Wookiee could move, the wampa raised a sleepy paw and pulled the furry Wookiee closer, **hugging** him like a stuffed toy.

Before Leia could think of a new plan, her comlink crackled to life.

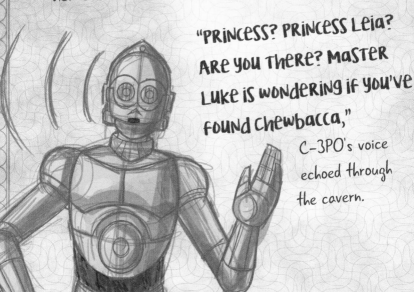

"PRINCESS? PRINCESS LEIA? ARE YOU THERE? MASTER LUKE IS WONDERING IF YOU'VE FOUND CHEWBACCA," C-3PO's voice echoed through the cavern.

Leia's hand dove to her comlink, frantically searching for the communicator's off button. **BUT IT WAS TOO LATE.**

The **WAMPA SNORTED AWAKE** and quickly realized that it had visitors. The beast lifted its paw to stand, and Chewbacca used the opportunity to twist out of its furry grip.

CHEWIE RAN TO LEIA AND C-3PO, AND THE THREE OF THEM BOLTED BACK TOWARD THE BASE.

Leia chanced a glance behind her, and saw the white beast thundering close behind them. **THEN LEIA REMEMBERED THE abandoned METAL DOOR SHE had SEEN ON HER way TO look FOR CHEWIE.** If they could bolt the door into its proper place, they would be able to stop the wampa from following them back to the base. The only problem was that it would take time to secure the door in place.

"CHEWIE, RUN AHEAD AND SEAL THAT PASSAGEWAY!" LEIA ORDERED. "I'LL DISTRACT THE WAMPA!"

Chewie didn't want Leia to get hurt, but he knew she could handle herself—even against a giant furry beast! The Wookiee picked up R2 and ran for the doorway.

Leia stopped to face the **CHARGING WAMPA**. In the bravest voice she could muster, she called, **"HERE, BOY!"** and ran in the opposite direction of Chewie and R2. As Leia sprinted away, the wampa went chasing after her. Its heavy feet thudded against the snowy tunnel floor. Each step brought it closer and closer to the princess. When it was almost within reach, it swung a clawed paw at her—**AND JUST MISSED, HITTING A COLUMN OF ICE INSTEAD!**

I wonder if wampas do not have the best eyesight? BUT IN THAT AREA, I CAN HARDLY JUDGE! I'M NEARLY BLIND WITHOUT MY GLASSES.

But where was I? Oh, yes! The fierce wampa was about to **CATCH THE PRINCESS**. Leia turned to face the beast, lifting her lantern high above her head. The wampa's fierce eyes caught the light, as he **SMASHED A PAW AGAINST THE LANTERN, KNOCKING IT INTO THE SNOW**. As the wampa turned to look down at the fallen object, Leia knew she had the perfect opportunity to run back to Chewie and R2.

She dashed forward toward the beast and slid right between its legs. **IT WAS TIME TO GET OUT OF THERE!**

She could see the Wookiee fastening the last bolt into place. Just then, she heard a **FURIOUS ROAR BEHIND HER**. The wampa was **NOT HAPPY** about Leia's tricky move! 20 meters, 15 meters, 10 meters . . . Leia was almost to the door when she saw a furry paw **SWIPE** down at her from the corner of her eye.

Leia dove to the ground and slid through the doorway. **"NOW, CHEWIE!"** she shouted.

CHEWIE SLAMMED DOWN ON THE CONTROLS AND THE DOOR SLID SHUT, LEAVING ONE VERY ANGRY WAMPA TRAPPED ON THE OTHER SIDE.

Leia breathed a sigh of relief. She didn't want to think about the half-a-million things that could have gone wrong, but hadn't. **Leia had been able to keep calm under pressure,** and even come up with a plan for the three of them to work together to escape the wampa.

Chewie pulled her into a **GIANT HUG,** and R2 beeped with excitement.

"You're welcome, Chewie," Leia said with a smile. "But I should say thank you, too. And Artoo. **Without your fancy tool work, I'd have been that wampa's dinner for sure.**"

It was not the sort of battle that would be celebrated for years to come. But the **LEADERSHIP** and **RESOURCEFULNESS** that Leia showed that day would serve her well in her fight against the Empire and other enemies for the rest of her life.

I, for one, was excited to watch on as she continued to lead in the galaxy. Maybe I'll even have some more stories to tell one day soon. . . .

SO YOU WANT ANOTHER STORY, EH? IT IS A GOOD THING FOR YOU THAT I AM SUCH AN EXCELLENT STORYTELLER.

This next tale is a good one. It is about a rebel **BOUNTY HUNTER** named

SABINE WREN.

Sabine was born on a planet called Mandalore. This planet was known for its **FIERCE WARRIORS** and tightly knit communities called "clans." Every Mandalorian was expected to be loyal to their clan, and the expectation for Sabine **WAS NO DIFFERENT.**

And so, when Sabine came of age and her parents sent her to an Imperial academy, Sabine went proudly. If becoming an Imperial officer was the best way for Sabine to serve her family, then she would do it, **and do it better than anyone.**

But when Sabine reached the academy, she found it hard to obey their rules. The Imperial officers tried to teach her to be **heartless** and **calculating,** focused only on the preservation of the Empire. Sabine had been trained from a young age to be loyal to her leaders,

yet she knew she could not serve the Empire.

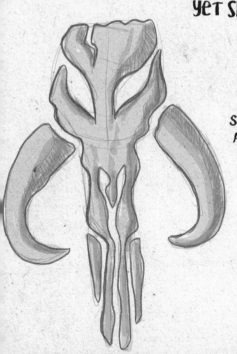

SOME MANDALORIAN ARMOR BEARS THIS DISTINCTIVE SKULL SYMBOL.

There was another girl at the academy, **KETSU ONYO,** who did not want to serve the Empire. Ketsu convinced Sabine to leave the academy and run away with her. They even decided to join a criminal group called **THE BLACK SUN** together. At the time, Sabine had thought the Black Sun was the best way for her to escape the Empire.

THE LEADERS OF THE BLACK SUN RULE FROM THEIR FORTRESS ON MUSTAFAR.

But as she and Ketsu **STOLE AND CHEATED** their way across the galaxy, Sabine realized that even though she was free, there were many others who still suffered under the Empire. Even worse, Sabine was doing nothing to help end that suffering.

Sabine knew she would never be truly free until everyone else was, too. **AND SO SABINE LEFT THE BLACK SUN AND KETSU BEHIND AND JOINED THE REBEL ALLIANCE.**

But Ketsu felt betrayed by Sabine's choice and refused to speak to her friend for some time after that.

I WONDER IF YOU HAVE EVER FELT LIKE SABINE?

Sometimes a friend might ask you to do something wrong. But if you close your eyes and listen, you will hear a voice encouraging you to stop. **THAT VOICE IS THE FORCE**, telling you what you already know in your heart. Like Sabine, you may worry that saying "no" to your friend will be disloyal, that you will have betrayed them. But how can anyone be truly loyal, if they have already betrayed themselves and what they know is right?

A REAL FRIEND WILL SEE YOUR CONVICTION, AND JOIN YOU.

Which is exactly what Sabine herself discovered. . . .

Sabine had a great gift for art, and she used that ability to bring color and beauty to everything around her— **even her hair!** On this day, it was a bright blue, and she was busy painting her new speeder bike to match.

What color should I try next?

Royal Blue

Forest Green

Teal and Orange

Bright Red

To Sabine, her art wasn't just a way to make something pretty. In a galaxy where the Empire wanted everyone and everything to be bland and identical,

SABINE'S BURSTS OF COLOR WERE AN ACT OF DEFIANCE.

As Sabine put the finishing touches on her speeder, her friend Hera came by to admire her work. "Are you ready to go on your mission?" Hera asked. "Ketsu will be waiting for you at the spaceport."

KETSU

Sabine was excited and nervous to see her old friend again. They had seen each other a few times since their big fight, and each time Ketsu grew closer to forgiving Sabine. Now Sabine only hoped that she could convince Ketsu to join her in her new life with the Rebellion. Sabine was encouraged that Ketsu had agreed to help her in her latest mission. **BUT WOULD IT BE ENOUGH TO CHANGE KETSU'S MIND?**

Sabine felt a knot of worry in her stomach as she boarded the **GHOST** with Hera and set course for Garel City.

Hera would drop Sabine at the spaceport and then wait for Ketsu and Sabine to complete their mission.

Sabine had stolen Imperial cargo countless times,

BUT THIS TIME WAS DIFFERENT.

HERA NOTICED HOW NERVOUS SABINE WAS.

"It is not always easy to convince someone to join the Rebellion, Sabine. Remember that. Remember how you yourself had to be convinced."

HERA ALWAYS KNEW THE RIGHT THING TO SAY.

Sabine nodded. "Ketsu is used to working alone, and only for profit. I don't know if she will give that up—YET."

Once she arrived at Garel City Spaceport, Sabine found a hiding place with a perfect view of the cargo bay doors. Inside was enough food to supply a small village for weeks. Leaning back against an empty crate, Sabine checked her chrono. Ketsu was late. **THE KNOT IN SABINE'S STOMACH GREW SLIGHTLY.** She decided to give Ketsu five more minutes, when she heard a soft thud behind her.

OH, I LIKE THAT STEALTHY KETSU! SHE HAD MANAGED TO SNEAK UP BEHIND SABINE WITHOUT HER NOTICING.

Sabine stopped herself from hugging her friend, and instead settled for a handshake.

"I didn't see you come in," Sabine whispered.

"THAT WAS THE POINT," Ketsu replied. "I've picked up a few tricks from Black Sun since we last met."

Sabine tried to ignore the Black Sun symbol on Ketsu's armor. Instead, she explained the plan to move the supply crates out from under the Empire's nose and into the landing bay. There, Hera would pick up the supplies, as well as Sabine and Ketsu.

Ketsu wrinkled her nose. "FOOD FOR THE REBELLION? I'll admit, THIS ISN'T THE KIND OF MISSION I had in MIND."

Sabine was frustrated by her friend's attitude. And yet Sabine recognized so much of the person she used to be in Ketsu. Perhaps that was a good sign that Ketsu would be able to travel the same path to the Rebellion.

"Well, it's not always about excitement," Sabine told Ketsu.

"SOMETIMES IT'S ABOUT HELPING PEOPLE IN NEED."

Ketsu didn't seem convinced, but Sabine didn't have time to argue with her. Instead, she motioned for Ketsu to follow her as she slowly crept though the maze of crates toward the cargo bay doors.

Once there, she inspected the thick durasteel frame and quickly spotted the control panel. Silently, Sabine drew her blaster and nodded to Ketsu to do the same. It felt good to be so in sync with Ketsu again.

IT REMINDED HER OF THE GOOD TIMES BEFORE THE BLACK SUN.

Sabine punched in the activation code, and the doors hissed open. The supply crate was just where Hera had said it would be—

BUT SO WERE AN ENTIRE TEAM OF STORMTROOPERS!

Those bucketheads know how to ruin a perfectly good mission.

In flawless unison, Sabine and Ketsu dove behind a nearby pile of metal panels and opened fire on the stormtroopers.

It only took a few minutes for Sabine and Ketsu to fight their way to the crate.

BUT SOMETHING FELT WRONG.

Why had the stormtroopers been centered around one crate of ordinary food?

As if in answer, one of the stormtrooper's blasts caught the edge of food crate, causing the front wall to fall open.

Sabine gasped at what she saw inside.
A little Chadra-Fan boy
was crouched within, clutching a half-eaten
ration bar in his hand. Sabine needed to
get the child to safety—and fast.

**But she was
pinned down
by enemy fire.**

To Sabine's
surprise, she saw
the dark blur of
Ketsu run toward the
crate without hesitation.
Sabine laid down covering fire, and within
moments Ketsu had recovered the child
and joined Sabine behind a particularly
sturdy crate.

The food would have to wait for a different mission. Now all that mattered was getting the boy to safety. Sabine privately noted that Ketsu hadn't even thought to save the food instead of the boy.

WHEN IT REALLY MATTERED, KETSU HAD CHOSEN TO SELFLESSLY SAVE SOMEONE ELSE.

Sabine knew Ketsu wouldn't want Sabine to call out her heroism. So instead, Sabine just smiled and said **"THIS EXCITING ENOUGH FOR YA?"** It is a sign of a good friend if they know when it is best to be serious, and when it is best to joke. And Sabine was a very good friend.

With the boy safe, Sabine pulled out her comlink and called Hera for backup. "SPECTRE-TWO! WE COULD USE SOME HELP IN HERE! THE MISSION'S GOTTEN A LOT MORE COMPLICATED!"

Hera punched the **GHOST'S** thrusters and headed straight for the cargo bay. She lowered the entry ramp and held the ship steady so that Sabine, Ketsu, and the boy could hop onboard.

"Go! Go!" Ketsu shouted. The three sprinted from their hiding place and leapt onto the *Ghost*. Chopper was standing by to raise the ramp behind them.

THE SECOND THE RAMP CLOSED, HERA FIRED UP THE ENGINES AND BLASTED OFF INTO SPACE.

Once they were far enough away, Sabine and Ketsu celebrated their successful mission. They may not have captured the supply crate, but they had managed to do something far more important by saving the Chadra-Fan boy.

"HOW DID IT FEEL FIGHTING FOR THE REBELLION?" Sabine asked.

Ketsu gave Sabine a look.

She knew her friend was hoping for a specific answer. But as Ketsu looked at Sabine, she felt the barriers she had raised around herself melt away.

"You know, it didn't feel all that bad. Being a part of something that fights for good. . . . It's been a long time. **TOO LONG, I THINK.**"

SABINE'S HEART LEAPT IN HER CHEST.

These were the words she'd been waiting to hear for years. When Sabine met Ketsu's eyes, she saw her own joy reflected there.

There was just one more thing to take care of. . . .
Sabine sent Ketsu to the common room and then ran to get her paint set. She had Ketsu chose her favorite colors, and then Sabine got to work painting over the Black Sun symbol on Ketsu's armor.

In its place, Sabine painted a yellow phoenix—the emblem of the Rebellion.

"IT'S PERFECT," Ketsu said.

This was how it was meant to be.

SABINE DESIGNED THE
SYMBOL FOR THE REBEL
PHOENIX SQUADRON.

Sabine offered Ketsu her hand.

"WELCOME TO THE REBELLION."

ISN'T IT WONDERFUL WHEN FRIENDS FIND EACH OTHER AGAIN? The Rebellion had shown that it was worthy of Ketsu and Sabine's loyalty—even if it took Ketsu a little bit longer to figure that out. **TOGETHER, THEY WERE STRONGER THAN THEY EVER COULD BE APART.**

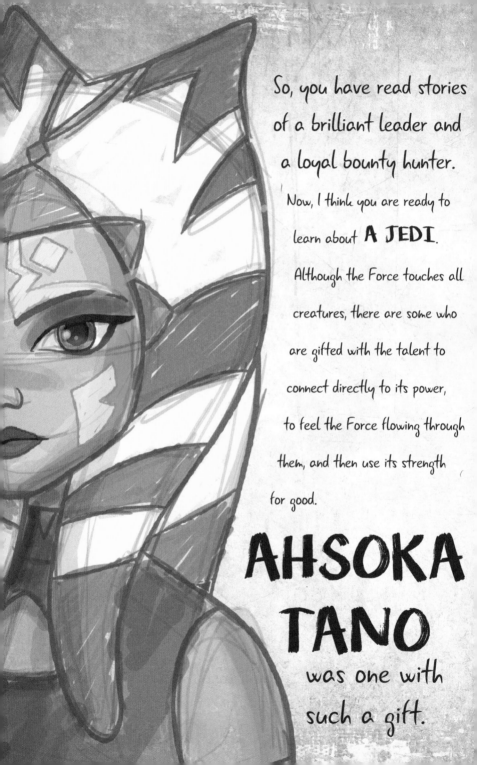

So, you have read stories of a brilliant leader and a loyal bounty hunter.

Now, I think you are ready to learn about **A JEDI**.

Although the Force touches all creatures, there are some who are gifted with the talent to connect directly to its power, to feel the Force flowing through them, and then use its strength for good.

AHSOKA TANO

was one with such a gift.

As a young child, it was clear that Ahsoka had a special relationship to the Force. She was sent to the Jedi Masters to help her study and **HONE HER ABILITY**. The Jedi believed that they must keep tight control over their emotions. It was only through peace and calm that a Jedi could hear and respond to the will of the Force. But Ahsoka's mind was anything but quiet. She had so many questions and even more ideas. She often acted impulsively, forgetting to think through the consequences of her actions.

IT WAS JEDI MASTER PLO KOON WHO BROUGHT AHSOKA TO THE JEDI ORDER.

When Ahsoka turned fourteen, **WISE MASTER YODA AND THE JEDI COUNCIL** decided she was ready to become a Padawan.

A Padawan was a young Jedi who trained closely with a **JEDI MASTER**. The Council always tried to pair the right master with the right Padawan so that they would bring out each other's **STRENGTHS**. But the Council made an unusual choice when it came time to select Ahsoka's master. They chose **ANAKIN SKYWALKER**, the most powerful Jedi to join the Order in some time. When he was only nine years old, he helped free the planet of Naboo from Trade Federation Forces. Later, he dueled with Count Dooku himself at the Battle of Geonosis. It was rumored he might one day become the youngest Jedi ever to be named to the Council.

Ahsoka understood that it was an **HONOR** to be Anakin's Padawan, but she was also a bit intimidated. If the Council had chosen such a **POWERFUL MASTER** for her, they must be expecting great things from her. She hoped she could live up to those expectations.

NOT AN EASY TASK!

Some days it seemed like the harder Ahsoka tried to do things right, the worse she muddled them up.

And today was no exception. It was the morning that Ahsoka was to receive her **NEW PADAWAN BEADS**—an important ceremony that symbolized her growth as a Jedi. She decided to stay up late meditating the night before.

She wanted her mind and heart to be in **PERFECT HARMONY** when Master Yoda performed the ceremony. Ahsoka stared at her meditation candle for hours, emptying herself of all **EMOTION**.

Slowly . . . slowly . . . her eyes began to droop, until she fell **FAST ASLEEP**.

She awoke the next morning
with a start and quickly checked
her chrono. **She was late!**
And on today of all days! Ahsoka
tried to focus on the positive—at least
she was already dressed for the ceremony.
She grabbed her lightsaber and ran out the door.

It was a busy morning on the streets of Coruscant.
I suppose every morning is a busy one on that giant city of a planet.
Ahsoka dodged a meiloorun cart as she **SPRINTED** toward the Jedi
Temple. Then the comlink on her wrist crackled with a familiar voice.

"Ahsoka? You on your way?"

It was Anakin's voice. And he did **NOT** sound pleased.

"I'M ON MY WAY, MASTER!
I JUST FINISHED PATROL."

Ahsoka told a white lie and hoped Anakin couldn't tell.

"Well, get back here, and hurry!" Anakin said. Ahsoka noted

that her master was **NOT EXACTLY THE IMAGE OF JEDI SERENITY**,

but since her tardiness was the source of his agitation,

she didn't mention it.

Ahsoka wiped the sweat from her forehead and continued **RACING** ahead. She was only a few minutes late. She could still arrive at the Temple with plenty of time left for the ceremony.

A moment before she heard the voice, she sensed something was wrong. **"NO! Oh, NO!"** The cry came from behind her—**away FROM THE TEMPLE.**

Ahsoka tried to push forward when the voice called out again. **"NOOO! GET away! SOMEONE hELP!"**

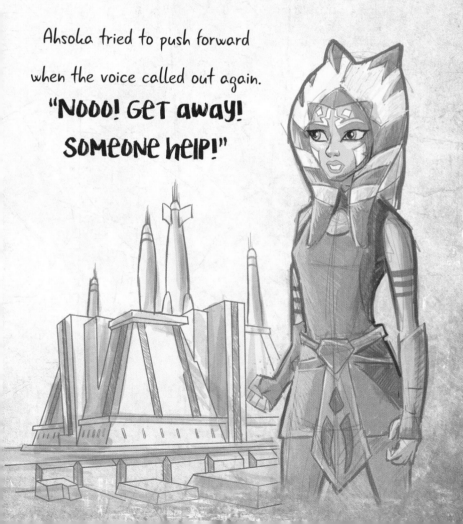

Ahsoka slowed down and turned toward the panicked voice. She might get in big trouble with Anakin, but she couldn't walk away from someone in need. She would just have to deal with the punishment later.

Ahsoka **darted** back the way she had come, weaving in between the busy vendors selling their wares. She didn't have to search long. A **stampede** of people was running away from the cries for help.

Take note, young one. The next time you see someone in trouble, watch to see who runs toward the problem and who runs away. You will find that it is much easier to hide among those who run away. But I hope that you will have the **courage** to join the **heroes** who run to danger. **Ahsoka was one of those heroes.**

Soon Ahsoka was close enough to see exactly what was going on. In a narrow alley, a construction droid was charging forward, **DESTROYING EVERYTHING** in its path. It's heavy arms waved wildly, **SMASHING** into walls and sending rubble flying.

Near its single red eye, Ahsoka spotted an open panel with sparking wires.

IT MUST BE MALFUNCTIONING!

THEY WERE ALWAYS A BIT STUFFY FOR MY TASTES,
BUT THEY CERTAINLY CARED DEEPLY ABOUT
BRINGING PEACE AND BALANCE TO THE GALAXY.

THE COUNCIL HELPED GUIDE THE JEDI ORDER FOR CENTURIES, AND ONLY THE GREATEST JEDI MASTERS WERE CHOSEN TO JOIN THEIR NUMBER.

Before Ahsoka could come up with a plan, she heard a frightened cry. The droid was headed straight for an Aleena woman and her young son. **THEY HAD NOWHERE TO RUN.** Ahsoka wanted to panic, to reach out wildly with the **FORCE** and sweep the droid out of the way. But using the Force out of fear could be just as dangerous for the family as the malfunctioning droid. Instead, Ahsoka fell back on her training. She instantly centered herself and raised a calm, steady hand toward **A NEARBY CARGO CRATE.**

The durasteel box flew forward,
PINNING THE DROID AGAINST THE ALLEY WALL.
The mother and child ran to safety,
leaving the alley clear.

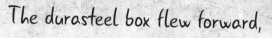

It wasn't long before the machine's glowing red eye
lOCKED ON TO Ahsoka. With a mighty heave,
the droid pushed the crate forward, freeing itself.
Although the droid wore no expression, Ahsoka could
tell that it was **NOT HAPPY.**

Ahsoka took out her lightsabers and ignited the blades. It was time to end this. **HER FIRST INSTINCT WAS TO RUSH FORWARD AND SLICE THE DROID INTO SCRAP.** She could feel every centimeter of the short space closing between them. It would only take a few seconds. . . .

She could feel the droid just on the other side of the durasteel wall. It would only take one swipe . . . **NO.** Ahsoka knew it was not the Jedi way to act impulsively. Instead, she looked around for more options. She was immediately rewarded when she spotted a leaking water pipe directly above the droid's head. **Ahsoka smiled.**

She leapt up, soaring high above the droid's head. In one smooth movement, she slashed through the pipe, **POURING WATER ONTO THE RAMPAGING DROID BELOW.**

As soon as the water touched its sparking wires, the droid began to **SMOKE** and **BUZZ.** It fell forward and its eye's glowing red light dimmed.

Ahsoka knew that with the droid shut down instead of sliced to bits, it could be repaired and return to work safely again . . .

NOT ENDANGERING THE CITY.

"THANK YOU FOR SAVING US," the young mother

called to her, with her son following closely behind.

"ARE YOU OKAY?" Ahsoka asked, patting the boy gently on

his head. The young Aleena nodded gratefully. Ahsoka looked back

to make sure the droid hadn't managed to reboot its system, and

then caught sight of the Jedi Temple spires in the distance.

**"THE
CEREMONY!"
SHE GASPED.**

AHSOKA HAD NEVER RUN SO FAST IN HER LIFE.

Each block flew by, until she was finally at the Jedi Temple. There, Anakin and Master Yoda were waiting patiently for her to arrive.

"SORRY—" Ahsoka gasped, **"I'M late."**

She bent down to catch her breath, her sweat mixing with the dried layer of dirty water that coated her from her montrals to her toes.

"Ahsoka, what happened?" Analin asked in concern. Ahsoka was relieved to see that his immediate reaction was not one of anger.

"LET'S JUST SAY ... THERE WERE SOME COMPLICATIONS." Ahsoka looked down at her boots, too ashamed to meet the Masters' eyes. Ahsoka didn't regret stopping to help the people in trouble, but she understood why Yoda and Analin must be furious with her.

They were silent for a moment, and then Ahsoka heard the gentle tap of Yoda's walking stick as he approached. He waited for her to look at him. When she did, Ahsoka was greeted with Yoda's broad smile.

"HUMBLE AND BRAVE, YOU ARE. A SIGN OF MATURITY, THIS IS...."

Ahsoka looked over at Analin in surprise. Her expression of shock was mirrored on Analin's face, but then her master began to glow with **PRIDE**.

Brimming with happiness, Ahsoka knelt before Yoda, and the old Master handed her her Padawan beads.

"OUTSTANDING GROWTH YOU HAVE SHOWN, AHSOKA TANO. ON THE PATH TO BECOMING A JEDI KNIGHT, YOU ARE."

Ahsoka took the beads in her hand and carefully clipped them to the jewelry string she always wore on her montrals.

She would remember that day for years to come, even as she grew to become a **POWERFUL WIELDER OF THE FORCE.** But she walked a different path than most Jedi. Her journey would not be simple or easy. Yet the choice to defy tradition if it meant helping others, would see her through even the most difficult of challenges. And I can say with certainty that Ahsoka's life was full of both challenges and victories.

THIS BEING JUST ONE OF THEM. . . .

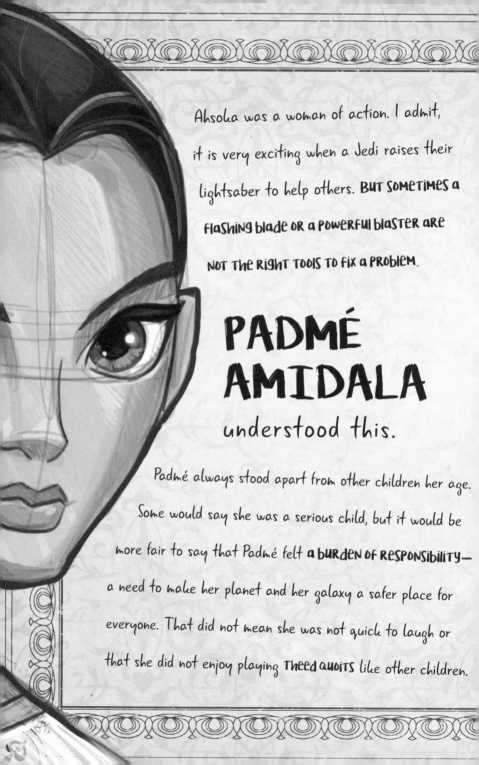

Ahsoka was a woman of action. I admit, it is very exciting when a Jedi raises their lightsaber to help others. **BUT SOMETIMES a FLASHING blade OR a POWERFUL blaster are NOT THE RIGHT TOOLS TO FIX a PROBLEM.**

PADMÉ AMIDALA

understood this.

Padmé always stood apart from other children her age. Some would say she was a serious child, but it would be more fair to say that Padmé felt **a BURDEN OF RESPONSIBILITY**— a need to make her planet and her galaxy a safer place for everyone. That did not mean she was not quick to laugh or that she did not enjoy playing **THEED QUOITS** like other children.

But she always put the needs of others before her own wishes.

Because of this, Padmé dedicated her life to **PUBLIC SERVICE,** and was elected Queen of Naboo at just **14 YEARS OF AGE.** But the life of a queen can be a lonely one. Padmé spent so much of her life serving others that she rarely had time for friendships. Padmé even held herself apart from her dear handmaidens, the brave young women who served as her counselors and bodyguards.

SHE KNEW EACH OF THEM WAS PREPARED TO GIVE THEIR LIFE FOR HERS.

And that is certainly a heavy weight on a **FRIENDSHIP.**

After fulfilling her role as queen, Padmé continued to serve as Naboo's senator to the Galactic Senate. Sometimes other senators would dismiss her ideas because of her age, but more often they would be impressed by Padmé's **POISE** and **INTElligence**. Soon, Padmé had become a respected voice in the government, responsible for negotiating agreements among even the most stubborn leaders.

One day, Padmé was organizing a diplomatic dinner, as she had done so many times before. But today she was worried. There had been several threats made against the Arthurian representatives. Padmé knew she couldn't risk anything going wrong at the meeting, so she went to the **Jedi TEMPle** to get help.

(I've had more than one experience with rowdy dinner guests, myself. I think Padmé made the right choice:

WHEN IN doubT, ASK A JEDI.)

Padmé took a deep breath, and then knocked firmly on the door to Ahsoka Tano's quarters. Ahsoka was the Padawan of Padmé's dear friend Anakin. [OF COURSE, YOU AND I BOTH KNOW THAT PADMÉ AND ANAKIN WERE MORE THAN JUST "DEAR FRIENDS," BUT THAT IS A STORY FOR ANOTHER TIME.]

Regardless, Padmé knew that **AHSOKA WAS A SKILLED JEDI** and would be able to help if any problems arose at the dinner. Ahsoka greeted Padmé warmly. "It's so good to see you, Senator. But I'm surprised YOU'VE come here to the Temple. Is everything all right?"

Padmé hoped that everything would indeed be all right. But it was **ALWAYS BEST TO PREPARE FOR THE WORST**. She explained the importance of the upcoming dinner and her fear that there might be an attack at the meal.

Ahsoka listened intently, touched that Padmé had asked for her help. **"I WOULD BE HONORED TO PROTECT YOU AND YOUR GUESTS,"** Ahsoka assured her.

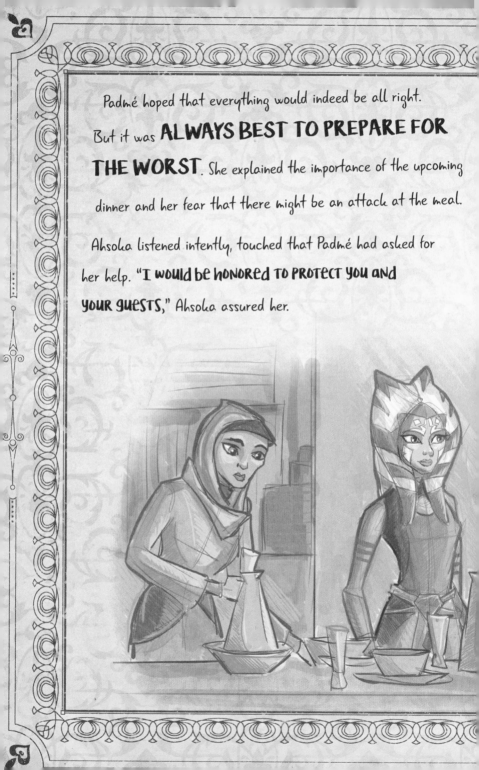

Padmé passed the next 24 hours finalizing all the preparations for the event. She made sure all of the Arthurians' favorite foods would be served and that **even the table decorations were to their tastes.** Now all that was left was to check in with Ahsoka about security. "Padmé?" Ahsoka called from the next room. "I just finished securing the outside of the building.

EVERYTHING IS CLEAR."

"I appreciate you helping me, Ahsoka," Padmé said.

"These negotiations with the Arthurian delegates are critical, and there are a lot of people who don't want them to happen."

Everything was ready. Now all Padmé could do was wait. It seemed like the right moment for Ahsoka to say her goodbyes, but Padmé wasn't ready for her to leave yet. She had to admit: **She didn't mind having someone her own age around for company.** She made a mental note to find ways to spend more time with the young Padawan.

"You know, it might not be such a bad idea if you stick around," Padmé suggested to Ahsoka. Ahsoka glanced around at each perfectly positioned decoration and the elegantly arranged meal.

"Thank you, Padmé. But it's not really my place to mingle with politicians."

Padmé skillfully hid her disappointment. "Next time, then. I insist."

Ahsoka bowed slightly, then headed for the door. As she passed the dinner table, Ahsoka paused for a moment to consider the place settings. Padmé tried not to get excited.

Perhaps Ahsoka had reconsidered staying?

"The table," Ahsoka said pensively. "Why did you set it with utensils? The Arthurian delegates never use them and might find it insulting."

Padmé hurried over to look at the offending cutlery.

"Hmm . . . you're right. And I was VERY SPECIFIC in my instructions."

SOMETHING WAS WRONG.

Padmé felt Ahsoka tense up and turn toward a nearby server.

Was she sensing something? "Excuse me," Padmé called to the server. "What is the meaning of this? **REMOVE THESE UTENSILS AT ONCE.**"

The server turned and drew a blaster. **PADMÉ'S EYES GREW WIDE**, and she felt Ahsoka pull her behind the table. The server fired directly where Padmé had been standing moments before.

R.S.V.P.

...midala of Naboo requests
...your presence at

...of Light Gala

...ellor Palpatine, and other notable
...celebrate the joyous anniversary
...to the Galactic Senate.

...tire Required.
...in Promptly at Dusk.

Senator Padmé A...

the honor o...

The Festival

Join Senator Amidala, Chan...
dignitaries from Naboo as u...
of Naboo's entry in...

Formal At...
Fireworks Will Be...

"Padmé? Is she on the guest list?" Ahsoka asked, already knowing exactly what Padmé's answer would be.

"NO, SHE'S NOT!" Padmé shouted. Ahsoka immediately ignited her lightsabers and began deflecting the attacking server's blaster bolts.

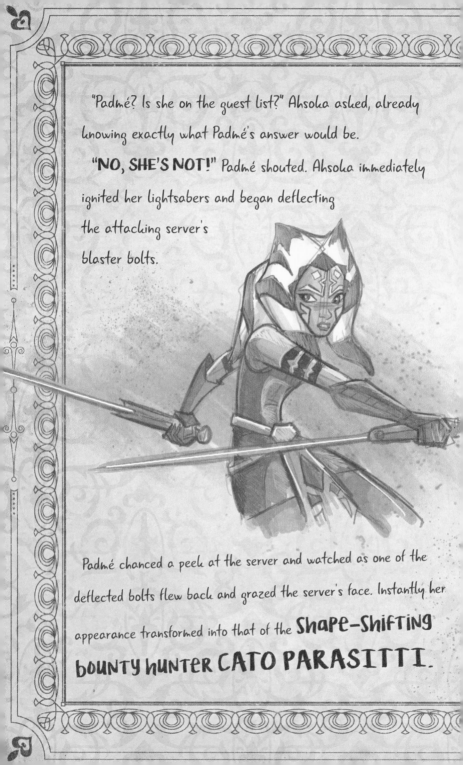

Padmé chanced a peek at the server and watched as one of the deflected bolts flew back and grazed the server's face. Instantly her appearance transformed into that of the **Shape-Shifting bounty hunter CATO PARASITTI.**

"**HOW DID SHE—**" Padmé started to say, but she was forced to duck as Ahsoka picked up a nearby chair and **THREW IT AT THE BOUNTY HUNTER.** Without her blaster, Padmé felt helpless to protect her friend. Not that Ahsoka needed any help, she was easily holding her own against Cato. Padmé decided the best thing she could do would be to run for help. She quickly crawled along the length of the table toward the front door. **ABOVE HER THE SOUNDS OF BATTLE HUMMED AND ZAPPED.**

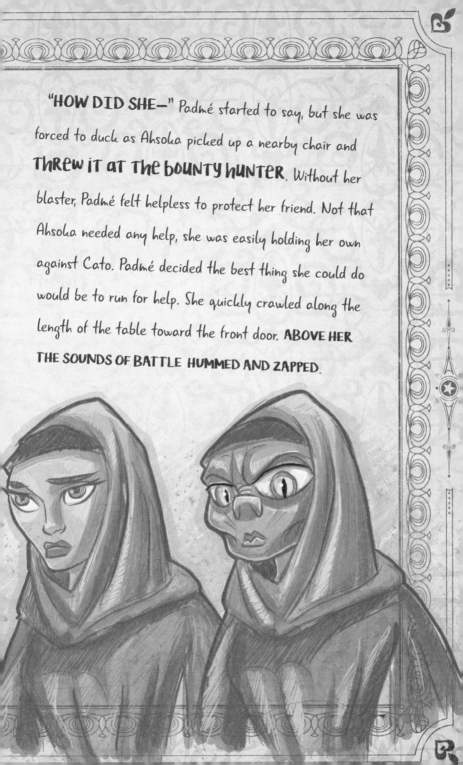

MISSION
OUTFIT

TRAVELING
GOWN

Headdress looks
formal, but
also saves time
hairstyling

all-weather
cape

comfortable
boots

loose robes

DRESSES AS DIPLOMACY

Whether negotiating an important treaty or meeting a high-ranking diplomat for the first time, appearances are important. By respecting the traditions of other planets and cultures, a good leader shows they are ready to listen and compromise.

QUEEN OF NABOO THRONE ROOM GOW

the Jewel of Zenda

hair styled in accordance with senate tradition

necklace given to Padmé by the Naboo Council

white nail polish

When Padmé reached the end of the table, she noticed a blinking metal dome attached to the table leg. As the lights started blinking faster and faster, Padmé immediately realized what it was.

"AHSOKA! THERE'S A BOMB!" she cried,

searching the dome frantically for a way to deactivate the device. But there was no way to remove it from the table without setting it off.

"SEND IT TO ME!" AHSOKA SHOUTED.

Padmé took a deep breath and kicked the table toward Ahsoka. The Padawan used both of her blades to cut a hole around the bomb, **THEN FORCE-PUSHED THE SWIFTIY blINKING dEVICE OUT THE CloSEST WINDOW.** Padmé barely had time to admire Ahsoka's quick thinking before an **EXPLOSION** lit up the outside sky.

Cato knew she had been defeated. The best she could hope for was a clean escape. **BUT PADMÉ HAD OTHER PLANS.** She grabbed one of the heavy vases from the floral displays and **SWUNG IT HARD** at Cato's face. The bounty hunter hit the floor, knocked completely unconscious.

Ahsoka rushed over to make sure Padmé was all right. But while Padmé's clothes might be a little rumpled, both she and Ahsoka had made it through the attack **WITHOUT A SCRATCH.**

"That was a nice trick there, with the vase," Ahsoka said, smiling. "You know, you remind me a lot of Anakin sometimes."

PADMÉ BLUSHED. IF Ahsoka ONLY KNEW.... Padmé looked everywhere else in the room but at Ahsoka. She was greeted with the sight of a completely destroyed dinner party.

"Well, it looks like these negotiations will have to be postponed." Padmé sighed. She hoped that Ahsoka would be free to help her with security then, too.

"In that case, I guess I will stay," Ahsoka said. **"I'd hate to see all that food go to waste."**

Padmé laughed and pulled an only slightly crushed jogan fruit from beneath the table. "Thank you, Ahsoka." She hoped the Padawan understood **SHE WAS GRATEFUL FOR MUCH MORE THAN HER PROTECTION TONIGHT.**

Heroes like Padmé often try to carry the weight of the galaxy on their shoulders. But a galaxy is much easier to carry **when you have a friend to help you do the lifting.**

I will be the first to admit that this is a very **easy thing** to say, and **a very hard thing to do.** Asking for help can be as terrifying as crossing the Jundland Wastes on a moonless night. But I think you'll find a true friend is always ready to lend a hand. And unlike in the Wastes, **you won't have to worry about krayt dragons attacking!**

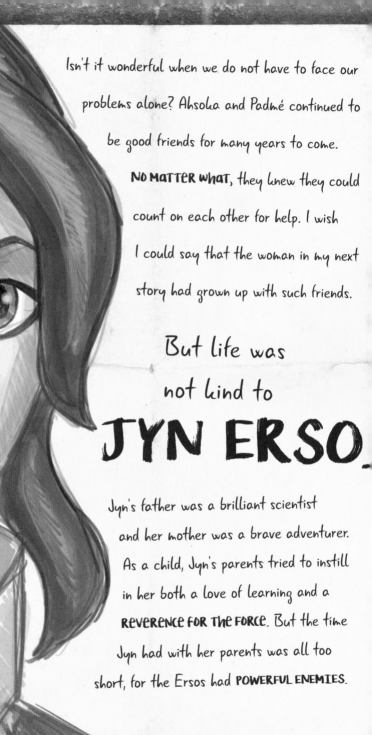

Isn't it wonderful when we do not have to face our problems alone? Ahsoka and Padmé continued to be good friends for many years to come. **NO MATTER WHAT,** they knew they could count on each other for help. I wish I could say that the woman in my next story had grown up with such friends.

But life was not kind to JYN ERSO.

Jyn's father was a brilliant scientist and her mother was a brave adventurer. As a child, Jyn's parents tried to instill in her both a love of learning and a **REVERENCE FOR THE FORCE.** But the time Jyn had with her parents was all too short, for the Ersos had **POWERFUL ENEMIES.**

Jyn's father had **REFUSED TO HELP THE EMPIRE** build a deadly weapon with the potential to DESTROY entire planets. The Ersos tried to hide from the Empire on a distant planet, and their plan did work for a time. For five beautiful years, the Ersos were happy. When the Empire did find them, they killed Jyn's mother and captured her father.

The duty of raising Jyn fell to Saw Gerrera, an old friend of the family. Saw was the best father he could be to Jyn, but his first priority would always be his fight against the Empire. And so, Saw did what he believed would be best for Jyn, he abandoned her. **AT 16 YEARS OLD, JYN WAS LEFT TO TAKE CARE OF HERSELF.**

BUT JYN WAS A SURVIVOR. She knew how to fight, how to win, and how to disappear. Over the years she created folders full of fake identities so that her enemies couldn't find her. Jyn could change her identity as easily as you or I might change our clothes.

WHEN YOU MUST ALWAYS PRETEND TO BE SOMEONE ELSE, IT GROWS HARDER AND HARDER TO REMEMBER WHO YOU TRULY ARE.

The sun was high in the sky as Jyn Erso walked through the market district of **GAREL CITY.** She was currently doing business under the name **TANITH PONTA.** Or was it **LYRA RALLIK?** Sometimes it was hard to remember who she was anymore. She pulled her scarf close around her face as she walked through the crowded streets. Stormtroopers were everywhere on Garel, and she couldn't afford to be noticed by the Imperial soldiers.

She scanned the crowd, looking for her contact. If she could pull off this deal, she'd have enough credits to **SLEEP IN A REAL BED** tonight. Jyn walked casually toward the meiloorun stand where the man had promised to meet her. Jyn decided to give him five more minutes, and then she was out of here. Even if the money was good, she couldn't spend credits from an Imperial prison.

"**THERE YOU ARE,**" a gravelly voice said behind her.

Jyn wanted to snap at him for being late, but she kept her calm.

"You got the credits?" she asked without turning around.

"What's the hurry?" the voice asked.

NOT A GOOD SIGN.

Anyone who wasn't itching to get off a planet crawling with stormtroopers was either a double agent or simply stupid.

"I have the documents, if that's what you're worried about." Jyn slowly turned around to look at the man. The details of his face were hidden behind his thick black cloak. He was **HUMANOID** in shape, but that was the most Jyn could tell. She held up the **datacube** she knew the man was after. **HE LUNGED FOR THE DOCUMENTS,** but Jyn pulled it back just in time.

"CREDITS FIRST," JYN SAID FLATLY.

But the man refused. He insisted she give him the datacube first, or he'd leave her with nothing. The thought of giving up her only bargaining chip **TERRIFIED** Jyn, but she didn't have much of a choice. She pressed the information into the man's hand and waited for her payment. The man examined the datacube until he was satisfied. Then he reached beneath his robes and pulled out a bundle of credits.

"TEN THOUSAND. JUST LIKE WE AGREED."

10,000 CREDITS WILL BUY YOU
PLENTY OF SPICED NYSILLIM TEA.

Jyn weighed the bundle in her hand. It felt right. Jyn nodded and watched the man slip away into the crowd.

She couldn't believe her luck. After so many troubles,

MAYBE THINGS WERE FINALLY STARTING TO GO RIGHT.

She made eye contact with the meiloorun vendor and asked to purchase one of the juicy fruits. For once, she could afford it.

"THERE SHE IS!"

a stormtrooper shouted as he pointed into the crowded square. Jyn's heart stopped cold as she clutched the fruit in her hand.

HOW COULD THEY HAVE FOUND HER?

But when Jyn turned to get a better look, she saw that

the stormtrooper wasn't after her at all. He and his partner

were threatening a young girl.

"PLEASE! LEAVE ME ALONE," the girl said.

It was only then that Jyn noticed her clutching a

tooka cat in her arms. But the stormtroopers

loomed above her. **"YOU ARE IN**

VIOLATION OF CODE

THREE-ONE-ZERO."

People from the market had begun to crowd around the soldiers and the little girl. It was the **PERFECT DISTRACTION**. Jyn could take her credits and get out of here without anyone noticing.

"SHE'S ALL I HAVE!" the girl's little voice hit Jyn all the way from the other side of the market.

"HAND OVER THE CAT," the trooper insisted, raising his weapon at the girl. Another trooper wrenched the cat out of the little girl's arms.

SPLAT!

Suddenly, a juicy meiloorun smashed into the back of the trooper's head. It took Jyn a few moments to realize she had been the one to throw the fruit.

The stormtrooper stood up and spun around furiously.

"WHO THREW THAT?" he demanded.

It was too late to turn back now. **"I did,"** Jyn said, stepping forward. **"I SUGGEST YOU PICK ON SOMEONE YOUR OWN SIZE."**

The troopers immediately took Jyn up on her offer.

The first soldier to reach her grabbed her by the collar.

HIS MISTAKE.

Jyn kicked him hard in the stomach, knocking him back into the other trooper. Jyn ran for the edge of the square, daring the stormtroopers to follow her. They foolishly took Jyn up on her offer.

As Jyn leapt over a storage crate, she glanced backward. Everything inside Jyn told her to just find a hiding place in which to disappear.

BUT THEY STILL had THAT little girl's cat....

Jyn turned to face the troopers and grabbed a pole leaning against a nearby tent. As the troopers tried to reach her, Jyn thrust the pole beneath one of the trooper's legs, forcing him to fall flat on his back. Jyn heard a frenzied meow as the cat leapt from the fallen trooper's arms and raced away.

Jyn grumbled, then followed after the terrified cat.

"GET HER!" one of the troopers shouted.

They began firing their blasters after Jyn.

Jyn couldn't get off a good shot and catch the tooka cat at the same time. But she needed to find a way to distract the stormtroopers. She kept one eye on the cat's bouncing purple tail as she searched for a solution. Her gaze landed on a leaking hot water pipe perfectly placed between her and the troopers. **SHE TOOK AIM AND FIRED** her blaster at the water pipe. As the bolt hit the pipe, she watched as it erupted into a cloud of dense steam.

CREDITS
(plus a separate pouch of credits in case her primary pouch gets stolen)

COMLINK

SCARF
perfect for cold weather AND hiding your face

THERMAL DETONATOR
(for emergencies only)

HER MOTHER'S NECKLACE
(with the kyber crystal)

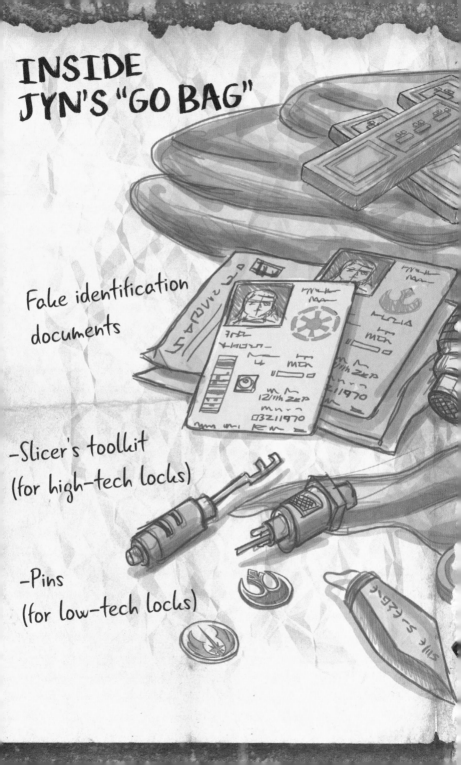

INSIDE JYN'S "GO BAG"

Fake identification documents

-Slicer's toolkit
(for high-tech locks)

-Pins
(for low-tech locks)

"WHERE IS SHE?" the stormtroopers shouted to each other. One of them called in two more soldiers to help. But Jyn knew even four stormtroopers were no match for her.

Jyn followed the cat back around behind the confused troopers. The animal was starting to get tired and was finally slowing down. If she could just get rid of the stormtroopers, she could grab the cat, return it to the girl, and get out of here with her cover intact.

Once again, Jyn scanned the market for something she could use to her advantage. But she didn't see anything this time.

Instead, **SHE HEARD SOMETHING.**

As Jyn's heavy boots thudded against something metallic, Jyn realized that there were grates scattered all over the market. They must lead to the sewer system below the city. . . . **AND ALL FOUR TROOPERS WERE STANDING OVER ONE OF THOSE GRATES.**

Jyn took aim and fired at the metal hinge holding up the grate beneath their feat. With a satisfying **CLANK!** the grate gave way and the troopers fell into the filth below.

"MEOW."

Jyn looked down too see the tooka cat rubbing its face against her legs. **TYPICAL TOOKA CAT.** Jyn quickly scooped up the animal and went to find the little girl. Jyn didn't want to admit it, but she was looking forward to seeing the girl's face when Jyn returned her pet.

"Tookie! You're back!" The girl's face split into a HUGE GRIN.

Jyn started to leave, when the little girl called after her. **"Wait!"**
Her eyes began to fill with happy tears. **"Thank you."**

Jyn nodded. Then, the girl asked her something that caught
her off guard.

"WHAT'S YOUR NAME?"

Jyn's mind immediately began flipping through her many aliases. But really, she was tired of running.

"MY NAME'S JYN ERSO,"

she said. And for the first time in a while, Jyn really did **feel like herself.**

My people have many stories about the power of names. Perhaps you have heard the tale of the Gungun who banished the evil Boss simply by speaking his secret name out loud? **NO?** Well, it is a good story—especially the way I tell it.

For now, I will tell you that by trusting the little girl with her true name, Jyn was reminded of the **KINDNESS** she had buried for many years. I hope you will never have to bury your heart as deeply as Jyn did. But if you do, I also hope that the Force will find ways to open your heart again.

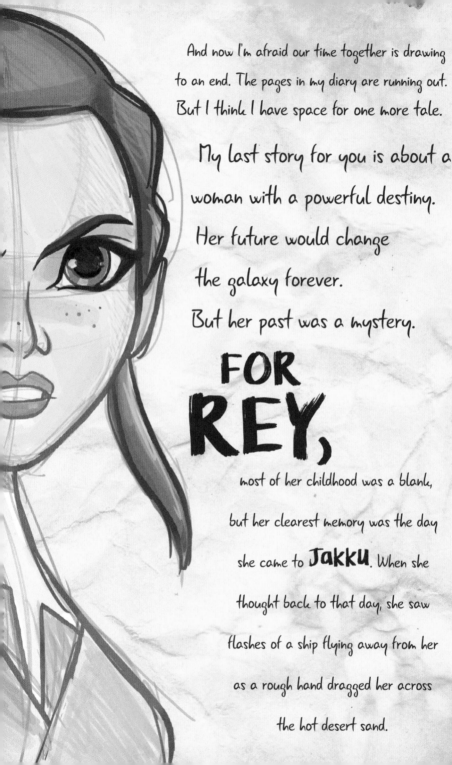

And now I'm afraid our time together is drawing
to an end. The pages in my diary are running out.
But I think I have space for one more tale.

My last story for you is about a
woman with a powerful destiny.
Her future would change
the galaxy forever.
But her past was a mystery.

FOR
REY,

most of her childhood was a blank,

but her clearest memory was the day

she came to **Jakku**. When she

thought back to that day, she saw

flashes of a ship flying away from her

as a rough hand dragged her across

the hot desert sand.

After that, the days began to blur together. She would wake up, search for salvage, and then trade whatever she found for food. Years passed in this way. Until the day when Rey meet a little round droid named

BB-8.

When Rey first saw the little droid trapped in the net of a Teedo, she had scared off the scavenger and freed the droid before thinking through the consequences of her choice. Rey had thought the droid would race off the second it was freed. **BUT INSTEAD, BB-8 had INSISTED ON STAYING WITH HER.** Rey eventually relented and told the droid he could tag along, but for one night only. **THE NEXT DAY, SHE WOULD BRING HIM TO NIIMA OUTPOST AND SEND HIM ON HIS WAY.**

BUT FOR TONIGHT, REY would have a GUEST IN HER HOME FOR THE FIRST TIME IN a long TIME. As the sun set in the distance, the sand was already beginning to cool beneath Rey's boots. They needed to get back to her home soon. The desert could be DANGEROUS AT NIGHT.

Rey glanced back and realized BB-8 WAS FALLING BEHIND as he struggled to roll across the shifting sand. She slowed down to give him a CHANCE TO KEEP UP.

"SORRY, little guy," she said. "I'M NOT USED TO WALKING WITH SOMEONE ELSE."

The droid beeped happily to himself, commenting on everything and anything they walked passed. Suddenly, BB-8 stopped and made a worried squeaking noise.

"Wait. What do you see?" Rey asked. But she didn't have to wait long to see what had frightened BB-8. Two red dots slithered silently across the sand, then disappeared. Rey recognized the monster immediately. It could only be a **NIGHTWATCHER.** The giant worms lived deep beneath the sands of Jakku, only surfacing to feed on the metal debris that dotted the planet's surface. Rey had never seen a whole nightwatcher before, but I certainly have.

Their long, purple bodies and sharp, spiny mouths **will give you nightmares for weeks!**

WITHOUT HER METAL SPEEDER, REY KNEW SHE WAS SAFE FROM THE WORM. BUT BB-8 WAS NOT. ONCE AGAIN, REY FOUND HERSELF RISKING HER SAFETY FOR THE LITTLE DROID. She had only survived on Jakku for so long by watching her own back.

She knew growing attached to others could be a weakness—
a painful lesson that Jakku had taught her many times.
And still, Rey got ready to defend BB-8. "Don't move," she cautioned
the droid as she reached for the staff on her back.

"That's a NIGHTWATCHER WORM. It feeds on junk."

BB-8 beeped indignantly at being called "junk," but he understood the warning in Rey's voice.

Rey remained completely motionless, straining to hear any sign of the beast. Sure enough, Rey heard a soft rumble as the sand beside them began to move. The nightwatcher's hideous head burst from beneath the ground and snapped hungrily at BB-8.

"NOW WE RUN!" Rey shouted. She could see the outline of her AT-AT home on the horizon. BB-8 wouldn't be able to run that far before the worm caught up to them.

"IT PROBABLY HASN'T EATEN TODAY," She shouted. "WE NEED TO FIND SOMETHING ELSE TO FEED IT!"

Rey glanced back to see how close the worm was. But Rey didn't see the beast anywhere.

Nightwatchers' Favorite Snacks
- Power converters
- Sensor dishes
- Speeder bike handles
- Dejarik Sets
- Pilex drivers

SUddenly, The NighTwatcher's scaly head shoT ouT
of The sand in fRONT of Them.
IT OPeNed iTs hoRRible mouTh and scReeched,
flickiNg iTs TONgues TowaRd BB-8.

(Yes, I wrote "tongues."
I warned you these
beasts are fearsome.)

BB-8 skidded to a stop
and sped backward as
fast as he could.

"Hey! OVeR heRe!" Rey shouted. As the
worm turned to face her, Rey jammed her staff
between its jaws, **locking** them open.

As the worm struggled to dislodge the staff, Rey and BB-8 raced toward the AT-AT. **"WE'RE ALMOST HOME!"**
Rey's celebration was cut short as she heard the terrifying sound of bending metal behind her. The worm's **POWERFUL JAWS** spat out Rey's staff, sending it flying through the air directly at her head.

Without thinking, Rey reached out her hand and caught the spinning staff out of the air.

IT FELT GOOD TO HAVE THE FAMILIAR BEAM BACK IN HER HAND.

THE WORM DIVED ONCE again beneath THE SAND, TRYING DESPERATELY TO CATCH UP TO THE LITTLE DROID.

Rey watched as **THE SAND RIPPLED**, reacting to the giant beast **THUNDERING BENEATH THE DUNES.**

Rey ran to the right, beating her staff against the sand in an attempt to distract the nightwatcher. But the swelling sand kept moving straight for BB-8. "WAIT! NO!" REY CRIED.

The worm's head erupted from the ground, grabbing BB-8 and pulling him back down beneath the grainy sand. Rey could hear the droids muffled beeping still coming from below her. If she acted quickly, there was still a chance to save him.

Rey closed her eyes and concentrated. Sometimes when Rey focused very hard she felt as if she could feel the energy of everything around her. Of course Rey dismissed this feeling as simply INTUITION. But you and I know that Rey was reaching out THROUGH THE FORCE. As she quieted her mind, she clearly saw the worm slithering beneath her. She raised her staff above her. Rey thrust her staff deep into the sand, striking the nightwatcher directly on the head.

The nightwatcher staggered under the sand, until it finally lifted its head to the surface and **SPAT BB-8 INTO THE AIR**. Rey ran forward and caught the droid, then closed the last few meters between her and her AT-AT.

The big beast watched them, still slithering slowly around where Rey had struck it. Rey saw the woozy worm. **SHE COULDN'T HELP BUT THINK IT LOOKED A LITTLE SAD**. The worm had only been trying to eat dinner, after all. Rey knew a thing or two about being hungry.

"**HERE**." Rey began pulling a few spare beams and panels off of the side of the AT-AT. "**TAKE THESE**."

The worm gratefully ate up the spare junk and then headed back down into the sand.

"WE'RE SAFE NOW," Rey promised BB-8. She gently wiped some of the worm's saliva from the little droid's eyepiece. BB-8 beeped in curiosity.

"HOW did I FIND YOU?"

Rey repeated his question. Rey thought about the feeling of peace and connection that had allowed her to hit the worm. The sensation excited her and terrified her at the same time. But now was not the moment to worry about such things.

Rey shrugged.
"I'M JUST lUCKY I gUESS."

HA! If Rey was "just lucky" then I am taller than a Wookiee. Which would be very convenient the next time I need to dust the tops of my shelves. But we both know that I am no bigger than an Ewok, and Rey was so much more than lucky.

It was not her power with the Force that made Rey a hero. Many cruel and terrible people can bend the Force to their will. **NO, REY WAS A hERO because She used That POWER TO help PROTECT The weak.** She showed compassion to those who might have been her enemies. And she faced danger with a courageous heart. Not bad for an orphan girl from Jakku!

Oh dear. It appears we have reached **THE END** of my stories for now.

I hope you enjoyed them.

No, more than that. I hope you **BELIEVED** them. I hope you read about the power of **LEADERSHIP, LOYALTY, PRIDE, FRIENDSHIP, TRUST,** and **BRAVERY,** and that you agree these abilities can change the galaxy.

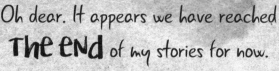

If you live long enough, you see the same eyes in different people. Each of these heroes came from different worlds—even different times. And yet they all shared the same fire in their eyes, the same **SPIRIT** that lead them to become forces of destiny. **IT IS IMPORTANT YOU KNOW: YOU HAVE THAT POWER,** TOO.

Studio Fun International
An imprint of Printers Row Publishing Group
A division of Readerlink Distribution Services, LLC
10350 Barnes Canyon Road, Suite 100, San Diego, CA 92121
www.studiofun.com

Written by Elizabeth Schaefer
Illustrated by Adam Devaney
Designed by Shaun Doniger, Jean Hwang, Kara Kenna, and Tiffany LaFleur

All notations of errors or omissions should be addressed to Studio Fun International,
Editorial Department, at the above address.

ISBN: 978-0-7944-4036-7

Manufactured, printed, and assembled in Stevens Point, WI, United States of America.

First printing, August 2017. WOR/08/17

21 20 19 18 17 1 2 3 4 5